Beauty
AND THE
Beast

Beauty
Lies
Within

Bath · New York · Cologne · Melbourne · Delhi
Hong Kong · Shenzhen · Singapore

This edition published by Parragon Books Ltd in 2016
and distributed by

Parragon Inc.
440 Park Avenue South, 13th Floor
New York, NY 10016
www.parragon.com

Once upon a time . . .

a beautiful girl named Belle longed to see the world beyond her quiet village. She spent her days reading stories filled with romance and excitement, hoping that one day she would have an adventure of her very own. When her father went missing, Belle left the village to search for him—and discovered a forgotten castle hidden deep in the woods.

The master of the castle was a bad-tempered, mysterious beast. Once a handsome young prince, the Beast had been transformed by an enchantress who cursed him for being vain and selfish—a curse that only true love could break. Taken prisoner in the castle, would Belle learn to see past the Beast's hideous appearance and discover his true inner beauty? Or would the Beast remain a monster forever?

Bring your own magic to every page of this delightful doodle book. Complete Belle's library, create an enchanted mirror, and use your creativity to bring the Beast's castle to life.

True beauty is found within.

Belle loves *to get lost* in a good story.

Doodle some *fairytale magic* on these pages.

Beautiful,
enchanted,
dangerous . . .

Add more
roses with
sharp thorns
to these pages.

Imagine a *mirror*
that could show you
anything....

What would you *wish to see?*
Doodle it in the frame.

Belle loves to read.
Color in the books
to complete her library.

Nothing in the **enchanted castle** is quite as it seems.

magical

UNFD

cursed

Add more
magical words
to this page.

Be our guest!
Belle finds new friends in the enchanted castle.

Fill in the petals
with
happy colors.

Belle looks beautiful in every color.

Doodle
a new pattern
for her dress.

Belle longs to *travel the world....*

Color in these pages *and* doodle some more ideas for *big adventures!*

The *enchanted castle*
is hidden deep in
the woods.

Add some tall trees
to hide it from
the outside world.

It's time for tea!

Help Mrs. Potts set
the table by
doodling
some
cups and saucers.

Beast and Belle
are having an
**enchanting
evening.**

Draw some more **guests dancing** around them.

Belle *loves all kinds* of flowers.

Fill these pages with *beautiful blooms.*

The **Beast's castle** is full of **old portraits.**

Draw the **Beast** as a **handsome prince** and add some more **portraits** to the castle walls.

Add
your own
inspiring
phrase to
this page.

And they all lived
happily
ever after.....